Against the Odds

Peter Conrad

Published by Peter Conrad, 2024.

AGAINST THE ODDS

First edition. November 19, 2024.

Copyright © 2024 Peter Conrad.

ISBN: 979-8230936541

Written by Peter Conrad.

Table of Contents

Against the Odds...1

A Love Remembered

The day Devon Walker entered the world was the happiest day of Marcus and Carol Walker's lives. Born at Harlem Hospital on a crisp November morning, Devon was the embodiment of hope and love in a world that often felt harsh and uncertain. Marcus, a janitor at Sutton Capital, had worked tirelessly to provide for his family. Carol, an elementary school teacher, was equally dedicated, not only to her students but also to the home they were building together.

Their modest apartment in Harlem was small, but it was filled with warmth, laughter, and the scent of Carol's home-cooked meals. She spent her evenings reading to Devon, instilling in him a love for learning that would last a lifetime. Devon thrived under her gentle guidance, absorbing every bit of knowledge she offered.

"Education is your key to the world, Devon," she would tell him, her voice soft yet firm. "No matter what anyone says, you're capable of achieving anything."

For Marcus, watching Carol interact with their son was like seeing magic. She had a way of making everything seem possible, of turning their modest home into a palace of dreams.

The Shadows Begin to Fall

WHEN DEVON WAS NINE, the first cracks appeared in their perfect world. Carol, always energetic and full of life, began to show signs of fatigue. At first, she brushed off her symptoms, insisting it was nothing more than a cold or the stress of teaching.

But Marcus noticed things he could not ignore. She would come home from work and head straight to bed, her meals untouched. Her laughter, once so frequent, grew rare. She hid her discomfort well, but Marcus could not shake the feeling that something was wrong.

One afternoon, Marcus decided to surprise Carol by coming home early from work. When he stepped through the door, the sight that greeted him froze him in place. Carol was curled up in bed, her face pale and etched with pain.

"Carol?" he said, rushing to her side. "What's wrong?"

She tried to wave him off, her voice barely above a whisper. "It is nothing, Marcus. I will be fine."

"No," he said, his voice trembling. "You are not fine. We are going to the hospital. Now."

The Diagnosis

AT THE EMERGENCY ROOM, a flurry of tests confirmed Marcus's worst fears. Carol had an aggressive form of cancer, and it had already spread to her liver. The prognosis was grim.

"There's nothing we can do except make her comfortable," the doctor explained gently, his words landing like hammer blows.

Marcus felt the world shift beneath him. He looked over at Carol, who was sitting quietly, her hands folded in her lap. She met his gaze, her eyes filled with a mixture of sadness and acceptance.

"I'm so sorry, Marcus," she whispered.

He knelt in front of her, taking her hands in his. "Do not apologize. We will get through this. Together."

At home, Marcus sat Devon down to explain what was happening. The boy's wide, innocent eyes filled with tears as he listened to his father.

"Your mom is sick," Marcus said, his voice breaking. "But we must stay strong for her. She needs us now more than ever."

Devon nodded solemnly, his small hand clutching his father's. "I will be strong, Dad. For Mom."

A Family's Final Months

THE MONTHS THAT FOLLOWED were a blur of hospital visits, quiet nights at home, and moments of unbearable heartache. Carol, ever the optimist, tried to make the most of her remaining time. She spent hours talking to Devon, reading to him, and encouraging him to dream big.

"Promise me you'll always do your best," she told him one night, her voice weak but steady. "No matter what, promise me you'll never give up on yourself."

"I promise, Mom," Devon said, tears streaming down his face.

Marcus, meanwhile, did everything he could to care for his wife and son. He worked long hours but always made it home in time to sit by Carol's side, holding her hand as they talked about the life they had built together.

Three months after her diagnosis, Carol passed away in her sleep. Marcus found her the next morning, her face peaceful, as if she had simply drifted off into a beautiful dream.

Devon, just nine years old, clung to his father as they mourned their loss.

"She loved us so much," Marcus said, his voice choked with emotion. "And we are going to honor her by living the best lives we can. That is what she would have wanted."

From that day forward, Marcus dedicated himself to raising Devon. Though the void Carol left behind could never be filled, her love and guidance continued to shape their lives. It was a love that transcended even death, a bridge that carried them through the darkest of times.

Sundays in the Park

AFTER CAROL'S DEATH, Marcus dedicated every spare moment to Devon. Though his job as a janitor required long hours, he made sure his son never felt neglected. Fortunately, Carol's sister, Deb, stepped in to care for Devon while Marcus worked. Deb, who adored her nephew, provided a loving presence that helped ease the boy through his grief.

But Sundays were sacred. No matter what was happening in Marcus's life, Sundays were reserved for Devon. It became their tradition to start the day with breakfast at a small diner on Lenox Avenue. Devon always ordered pancakes with extra syrup, and Marcus would have eggs and toast.

After breakfast, they would walk to a small park on 135th Street behind Harlem Hospital. The park was quiet in the early morning, often empty except for the two of them. It was their sanctuary, a place where they could talk, laugh, and simply be together.

A Morning on the Court

ONE SUNDAY, AFTER THEIR usual game of shooting hoops on the worn basketball court, they sat on a bench facing the towering handball wall. The wall, cracked and weathered, loomed large against the quiet morning.

"Dad, what's that wall for?" Devon asked, pointing to it.

Marcus smiled, his face lighting up with a mix of nostalgia and pride. "That's a handball court," he said. "It was popular when I was your age. A lot of guys used to play it, but you do not see many people using it now."

Devon tilted his head, intrigued. "How do you play handball?"

Marcus leaned back on the bench; his eyes distant as he recalled his younger days. "Handball is a lot like tennis, but without a racket. You use your hand to hit the ball against the wall, and the goal is to outsmart your opponent. It is not just about speed or strength—it is about strategy. It is like tennis and chess rolled into one."

Devon's eyes widened. "You played handball?"

Marcus nodded, a proud smile spreading across his face. "I did not just play, son. I was one of the best in the neighborhood. While most of my friends were shooting hoops, I was on the handball court. I loved the challenge, the focus it needed. It is you against the wall, trying to expect your opponent's next move."

"Can you teach me?" Devon asked eagerly.

Marcus laughed softly. "I do not know if my hands are what they used to be, but sure, I will teach you. It is a great game, and I think you would be good at it."

Lessons on and off the Court

OVER THE NEXT FEW SUNDAYS, Marcus began teaching Devon the basics of handball. They practiced hitting the ball against the wall, and Devon quickly noticed the nuances of the game.

"It's not just about hitting the ball hard," Marcus explained during one lesson. "You must think a few steps ahead. If you hit it here—" he pointed to a spot on the wall, "—where will your opponent be? Where do you want the ball to go next? Always be thinking, always be planning."

Devon listened intently, his young mind absorbing not just the rules of the game but also the lessons behind them.

Handball became more than a game for them. It was a way for Marcus to connect with his son, to pass down not just a skill but also a mindset. "Life's a lot like handball," Marcus said one morning as they packed up to leave the park. "You'll face challenges, but if you stay focused and think ahead, you'll find a way to win."

Devon looked up at his father, his admiration clear. "I'll remember that, Dad."

Building Memories

THOSE SUNDAY MORNINGS in the park became a cornerstone of Devon's childhood. Even as he grew older and their lives became more complicated, he would always look back on those moments with gratitude. They were not just learning a game—they were building a bond that would carry them through life's difficulties.

For Marcus, those Sundays were a chance to give his son something beyond the material—something that could not be measured in dollars or possessions. It was time, wisdom, and love.

And for Devon, they were a reminder that even in the face of loss and hardship, he was never alone. His father was always there, guiding him, one bounce of the ball at a time.

Loss and Resilience

DANIEL SUTTON GREW up in a home filled with love, discipline, and a strong work ethic. His father, John Sutton, had built Sutton Capital from the ground up, transforming it into one of the most respected firms in the country. John was a hard-working but deeply ethical man, supported every step of the way by his devoted wife, Kathren, whom he lovingly called Katie.

John and Katie had only one child, Daniel, who was the light of their lives. Though they loved him deeply, they were determined not to spoil him. John instilled the same sense of responsibility and discipline in Daniel that his own father had instilled in him.

Growing up in this nurturing environment, Daniel developed a deep respect for hard work and integrity. He excelled in school, and the pride in John's eyes was unmistakable when Daniel announced that he had been accepted to Harvard.

At Harvard, Daniel thrived. He studied business and finance, eventually earning a law degree. It was during his time there that he met Elizabeth, a bright and beautiful woman who would become the love of his life.

Building a Family

AFTER GRADUATING, DANIEL and Elizabeth returned to live with John and Katie at the Sutton estate. Elizabeth quickly became a beloved member of the family, and John and Katie treated her as their own daughter.

A little over a year later, Elizabeth gave birth to Ella, their first child. John, who had always believed in the importance of discipline and humility, found himself utterly captivated by his granddaughter. From the moment he held Ella in his arms, she had him wrapped around her finger.

Two years later, the family welcomed Elliott. The joy of having a grandson mirrored the delight they had felt with Ella's arrival. The Sutton family had it all—love, success, and a shared commitment to their values.

After John and Katie passed away, Daniel poured himself into expanding Sutton Capital, while Elizabeth focused on raising their children. Although the Sutton household employed a staff of housekeepers, gardeners, and a chauffeur, Elizabeth insisted on doing many things herself. She loved to cook for her family and cherished her morning rituals with Ella, especially their Saturday trips into the village to grocery shop and explore the local boutiques.

The Morning Everything Changed

ONE SATURDAY MORNING, Elizabeth awoke early, kissed Daniel, and whispered for him to sleep in. He had endured a grueling week at work and needed the rest. She and Ella quietly slipped out of the house, climbed into their Mercedes, and set off on their usual routine.

As the hours passed, Daniel did not think much of their absence. He assumed Elizabeth and Ella were simply enjoying their time together, wandering from shop to shop.

But then the phone rang.

The call came from the main gate, where two detectives were waiting to speak with Daniel. Puzzled and slightly uneasy, Daniel descended the grand staircase of the estate, his footsteps echoing against the marble floors. From the top of the steps, he watched the detectives' car wind up the long driveway, finally stopping in front of the mansion.

The two officers stepped out of their vehicle: their faces somber. They climbed the steps and introduced themselves before delivering the news that would shatter Daniel's world.

"There was a car accident," one of the detectives began. "Your wife and daughter didn't survive."

The words hung in the air like a heavy, suffocating fog.

Daniel staggered backward, his face pale, his breath caught in his throat. Then, with a heart-wrenching scream, he collapsed to his knees. The sound of his anguish filled the expansive space of the entryway, reverberating off the marble walls.

Elliott, who had been playing upstairs, came running at the sound of his father's cry. He reached the landing and froze, taking in the scene before him: his father, crumpled on the floor, tears streaming down his face, clutching at his chest as if the pain were too much to bear.

"Dad!" Elliott shouted, rushing to his father's side.

Daniel pulled his son into a tight embrace, holding him as if letting go would mean losing him, too. Together, they cried—father and son, bound by a grief so profound it seemed impossible to endure.

The Days That Followed

THE DAYS AFTER THE accident were a blur for Daniel and Elliott. The Sutton estate, once filled with laughter and warmth, now felt cold and hollow. Friends and family came and went, offering their condolences, but nothing could fill the void left by Elizabeth and Ella.

Daniel, who had always been a pillar of strength, struggled to find his footing. He had lost not only his wife but also the daughter who had brought so much light into their lives. Yet, even in his darkest moments, he knew he had to be strong for Elliott.

"Your mom and Ella wouldn't want us to give up," Daniel told his son one evening as they sat together in the quiet of the estate. "We have to keep going—for them."

Elliott, still so young, nodded solemnly, clinging to his father's words.

The loss of Elizabeth and Ella changed Daniel forever. It deepened his resolve to honor the legacy of his parents and to build a life that would make his family proud. But it also left a wound that would never fully heal—a reminder of the fragility of life and the profound love he had lost.

A Friendship Born in Late Nights

In the towering Midtown Manhattan building that housed Sutton Capital, the nights often stretched long for Daniel Sutton. While most employees left promptly at 6 PM, Daniel's office light would remain on, illuminating spreadsheets, prospectuses, and the ambitious dreams of a man determined to build an empire.

It was during one of these late nights that Daniel first met Marcus Walker. Marcus, the janitor assigned to the executive floor, was a quiet presence, meticulously cleaning offices and emptying trash bins without drawing attention to himself.

At first, their interactions were brief nods of acknowledgment or a polite "good evening." But as the weeks turned into months, the two men began exchanging words. Marcus would pause during his rounds to comment on the city's unrelenting noise or ask Daniel how his night was going.

"Burning the midnight oil again, Mr. Sutton?" Marcus asked one evening as he wiped down the glass doors of the conference room. Daniel looked up from his desk, smiled.

A Bond Forged in Loss

ONE NIGHT, AS DANIEL Sutton leaned back in his chair, rubbing his temples after hours of poring over financial reports, Marcus Walker entered the office to empty the trash. It had become their routine to exchange a few words during these late hours, but tonight, Daniel noticed something different about Marcus—a heaviness in his eyes, as though the weight of the world rested on his shoulders.

"You are alright, Marcus?" Daniel asked, setting down his pen.

Marcus hesitated, the trash bag in his hands crinkling as he paused. "Just a lot on my mind, Mr. Sutton."

Daniel leaned forward. "You have been working here for years, Marcus. Call me Daniel. And if there is something weighing on you, I am happy to listen. Sometimes talking helps."

Marcus glanced around the empty office and then lowered himself into one of the guest chairs across from Daniel. It was not his usual style to share personal matters, especially not with someone like Daniel Sutton, but there was a sincerity in Daniel's tone that disarmed him.

"I lost my wife three years ago," Marcus began, his voice quiet. "Cancer. She fought it hard, but..." He shook his head, swallowing the lump in his throat. "She didn't make it."

Daniel's face softened. "I am so sorry, Marcus. I cannot imagine how hard that must have been."

Marcus nodded, his hands gripping the edges of the chair. "It is just me and my boy now. Devon. He was ten when it happened. Smart kid, but it has been tough. I try to be there for him, but between school, work, and just... life, some days it feels like I am failing him."

Daniel leaned back, studying Marcus with a new sense of respect. "Raising a child on your own is no small thing. You are doing more than most people would in your situation."

Marcus chuckled, though it lacked humor. "I do what I can, but cleaning offices does not exactly pay enough to give him the life I want for him. He deserves more. She—my wife—always said Devon would do important things. I just hope I can help him get there."

Daniel nodded thoughtfully. "It sounds like you are doing more than you give yourself credit for. Providing for him, being there for him—that is what matters. And I have seen how hard you work, Marcus. That kind of determination? It gets noticed."

The two men sat in silence for a moment, the hum of the city outside the only sound between them. For Daniel, Marcus's story struck a chord. Though their lives were worlds apart, Daniel recognized the same drive in Marcus that had fueled his own rise in the financial world—the unyielding determination to build something greater for the people they cared about.

"Marcus," Daniel said after a long pause, "if there is ever anything I can do to help, let me know. Devon deserves every chance to succeed, and I mean it when I say you are one of the hardest-working people I have met."

Marcus smiled, the first genuine smile in what felt like days. "Thank you, Daniel. That means more than you know."

From that night on, their relationship deepened. What had started as casual late-night conversations grew into a genuine friendship. Daniel began to see Marcus not just as the janitor cleaning his office but as a man of resilience and quiet strength—a kindred spirit in many ways.

This bond would later shape the course of both their lives, leading to an unexpected partnership that would forever intertwine their families.

Betrayal and a New Opportunity

IT STARTED WITH TRIVIAL things; the kind Daniel Sutton could easily overlook. A missing bottle of expensive scotch from his private bar. Gas receipts that did not match the miles logged on the car. A few odd discrepancies in the petty cash he gave his chauffeur, Roy Sullivan, for errands. Daniel had always been a trusting man, to a fault, but as these small irregularities began to pile up, he decided to dig deeper.

One evening, Daniel returned home earlier than usual from a meeting to find Roy lounging in the backseat of the Bentley, parked in the driveway, smoking a cigar. Next to him sat a shopping bag filled with designer clothes—clothes Daniel knew he had not asked for.

"Roy," Daniel said, stepping out of his car and gesturing toward the bag, "mind explaining this?"

Roy stammered, quickly putting out the cigar. "Oh, uh—these are for you, Mr. Sutton. Just thought I would pick up some extras for you on my way back."

"Extras? With what money?" Daniel asked sharply.

Roy's face paled, and the weak excuse crumbled under Daniel's glare. Realizing he had been caught, Roy tried to talk his way out of it, but it was too late. Daniel dismissed him on the spot, furious at the betrayal.

The incident left Daniel shaken, not just because of the theft but because Roy had been with him for years. Trust, Daniel realized, was a fragile thing. He needed someone who would not just drive him from point A to point B but someone dependable, loyal, and honest.

The Offer to Marcus

THE NEXT NIGHT, AS he worked late in his office, Marcus Walker came in for his usual rounds. Seeing Daniel looking more worn than usual, Marcus hesitated before speaking.

"Rough night, Mr. Sutton?" Marcus asked.

Daniel sighed, rubbing his temples. "You could say that. Just found out my chauffeur's been stealing from me for God knows how long."

Marcus shook his head. "That is tough. Hard to find people you can trust these days."

Daniel looked at Marcus thoughtfully, the wheels turning in his mind. He had known Marcus for years now. The man was hardworking, honest, and carried himself with quiet dignity. More importantly, Marcus was raising a son on his own, juggling two jobs just to make ends meet.

"Marcus," Daniel said after a long pause, "how would you like a change of pace?"

Marcus frowned. "What do you mean?"

"I need a new chauffeur," Daniel explained. "But I do not just need someone to drive me around. I need someone I can trust—someone who is dependable. You have been working here for years, and I have never met anyone who takes their job as seriously as you do."

Marcus's brow furrowed. "I appreciate the offer, Mr. Sutton, but I am not sure I am cut out for that kind of job. Driving's one thing, but being a chauffeur..."

Daniel waved him off. "The driving's the easy part. And you would be more than just a chauffeur, Marcus. You would be part of the household. You and Devon could move into the guest house on the estate. It is nothing fancy, but it is better than where you are living now. Devon would have space to grow, and you would have more time for him."

Marcus sat down, stunned by the offer. "Why would you do this for me?"

Daniel leaned forward, his voice steady. "Because I see how hard you work, Marcus. I see the sacrifices you have made for your son. And because I trust you. I know you will not take advantage of this opportunity."

Marcus hesitated. The idea of uprooting his life was daunting, but the thought of giving Devon a better future outweighed his doubts.

"I'd have to talk to Devon," Marcus said finally. "But... thank you, Mr. Sutton. This means more than I can say."

Daniel smiled. "Take your time. And remember, call me Daniel."

A New Beginning

WITHIN A WEEK, MARCUS and Devon moved into the Sutton estate. The guest house, though modest by the standards of the palatial property, was more than Marcus could have hoped for. Devon, initially shy and unsure of the change, quickly grew to love the sprawling grounds.

For Marcus, the role of chauffeur was not just a job—it was a chance to rebuild his life, provide stability for his son, and repay the trust Daniel had placed in him. What neither man realized at the time was how deeply this decision would intertwine their lives, setting the stage for triumphs and conflicts neither could have predicted.

The First Introduction

A FEW WEEKS LATER, after offering Marcus the chauffeur position, Daniel decided it was time to introduce Marcus and Devon to Elliot. It was a Saturday afternoon, and Daniel invited Marcus to bring Devon to the estate to settle into the guest house.

Elliot had been sulking on the front steps of the main house, earbuds in, scrolling through his phone. He looked up briefly as a modest sedan pulled into the long driveway. Marcus stepped out first, looking a little overwhelmed by the grandeur of the estate. Then Devon appeared, holding a worn backpack.

"Elliot!" Daniel called from the porch. "Come over here and meet someone!"

Reluctantly, Elliot pulled out his earbuds and shuffled over, his sneakers scuffing the stone path. He eyed Marcus and Devon curiously but said nothing.

"This is Marcus," Daniel said, placing a hand on Marcus's shoulder. "He will be working with us. And this is his son, Devon. Devon, meet my son, Elliot."

Devon offered a polite nod. "Hi."

Elliot gave a half-smile, hands stuffed in his pockets. "Hey."

There was an awkward pause before Daniel clapped his hands together. "Why don't you show Devon around, Elliot? Maybe take him down to the basketball court or something?"

Elliot sighed but nodded. "Sure. Come on."

Devon hesitated, glancing at his father, who gave him an encouraging nod. Then he followed Elliot down the path toward the back of the house.

The Start of Something New

AS THE BOYS DISAPPEARED, Marcus turned to Daniel, a mix of gratitude and unease on his face. "Thank you, Mr. Sutton. For this opportunity—for everything. I do not know how I will ever repay you."

Daniel shook his head. "You do not have to. Just keep being the man you are, Marcus. That is repayment enough."

From the basketball court, the faint sound of laughter drifted back toward the two men. For the first time in a long time, Marcus allowed himself to hope.

Elliot and Devon: A Friendship Through the Years

FROM THEIR FIRST MEETING, Elliot Sutton and Devon Walker forged a tentative connection that quickly blossomed into a genuine friendship. At first, it was the shared novelty of having someone their own age on the vast estate that drew them together. Elliot, the restless and energetic son of wealth, was intrigued by Devon's quiet intelligence and grounded demeanor. Devon, in turn, was fascinated by Elliot's carefree confidence and the privileges of a world he had only seen from the outside.

Shared Adventures

OVER THE YEARS, THE boys became inseparable. Whether it was racing bikes on the estate's sprawling grounds or playing basketball on the court behind the mansion, their days were filled with shared laughter and spirited competition. Elliot introduced Devon to luxuries he had never experienced before—video games in the ultramodern game room, swimming in the estate's infinity pool, and occasional rides in the family's luxury cars.

Devon, meanwhile, brought a fresh perspective to Elliot's life. He was a voracious reader and had an uncanny ability to solve problems, whether it was fixing Elliot's bike or helping him study for a math test. Elliot often joked that Devon was like a walking encyclopedia, but he also deeply admired his friend's intellect.

"Why do you even bother hanging out with me?" Elliot said one day, sprawled on the grass after a game of soccer. "You're smarter than half the kids in my school."

Devon shrugged. "You're not so bad, even if you are kind of lazy."

Elliot laughed, tossing a blade of grass at him. "You keep me in check, Walker."

Subtle Differences Begin to Emerge

AS THEY GREW OLDER, Devon noticed the subtle ways their lives diverged. While Elliot's world was filled with lavish birthday parties, designer clothes, and weekend trips to exclusive resorts, Devon's life remained tethered to the guest house and his father's duties.

At first, Devon did not mind. He loved the Sutton estate and the opportunities it afforded him. But as they entered their teenage years, the disparities became harder to ignore.

One evening, after a particularly heated basketball game, Elliot casually mentioned plans to attend a private summer camp in Switzerland.

"You should come," Elliot said, wiping sweat from his brow. "It'd be awesome."

Devon hesitated, knowing full well that his father could not afford such an extravagant trip. "Yeah, maybe," he said, trying to keep the disappointment out of his voice.

Elliot did not notice. "We will have to convince my dad to bring you along. He is cool about stuff like that."

Devon nodded but did not say anything more. He was not sure how to explain to Elliot that his father's generosity, while appreciated, did not erase the reality of their unequal circumstances.

A Pivotal Moment

THE TURNING POINT CAME when the boys were sixteen. Elliot had invited a group of friends from his prestigious prep school over for the weekend. Devon, excited at first, quickly realized he did not fit in.

During lunch, one of Elliot's friends made an offhand remark about "the help" while complaining about the service at a restaurant. Devon froze, the words hitting him like a slap.

Elliot, oblivious to the impact of the comment, laughed along with the others. Devon excused himself shortly afterward, retreating to the guest house.

That evening, Elliot found him sitting on the steps outside, staring out at the driveway.

"Hey," Elliot said, sitting down beside him. "What up? You have been quiet all day."

Devon shrugged. "Nothing. Tired."

Elliot frowned. "Come on, Devon. I know you better than that."

Jamal hesitated, then finally spoke. "It is just... sometimes I feel like I do not belong here. Like no matter how close we are, I will always just be the chauffeur's son."

Elliot looked at him, startled. "That's not how I see you."

"Maybe not," Devon said, his voice steady, "but it is how the world sees me. And it is different for you, Elliot. You do not have to think about stuff like that."

Elliot was silent for a long moment, clearly grappling with the realization. "I don't care what other people think," he said finally. "You are my best friend. That is all that matters."

Devon appreciated the sentiment, but deep down, he knew their friendship could not shield him from the realities of their different worlds.

Drifting Paths

BY THE TIME ELLIOT left for boarding school, the boys' friendship had begun to change. While they still cared deeply for each other, their paths were diverging. Elliot was immersed in the privileged world of private education and international connections, while Devon focused on excelling at his public high school and helping his father as his health began to decline.

Devon poured himself into his studies, determined to carve out a future for himself that was not defined by the limitations of his upbringing. But the differences between him and Elliot—between the life of a wealthy heir and the son of a hardworking chauffeur—stayed a quiet but persistent wedge in their friendship.

Though the bond they had formed as boys would never truly fade, Devon could not shake the feeling that he was destined to walk a different road, one where he would have to work twice as hard to prove his worth in a world that was not built for him.

Marcus Walker's Declining Health

AS THE YEARS PASSED, Marcus Walker stayed a pillar of strength and reliability in the Sutton household. He took immense pride in his role as the family chauffeur, not just because it provided for Jamal but because it gave him a sense of purpose and belonging. However, his once-strong physique began to falter in subtle, troubling ways.

It started with bouts of coughing that he dismissed as nothing more than a lingering cold. Then came the fatigue. Long drives into the city became more taxing, and tasks that once seemed effortless now left him short of breath. Devon noticed the changes, too—the way his father winced as he climbed into the car or the faint wheezing that followed him up the stairs of their guesthouse.

"You need to see a doctor, Dad," Devon said one evening, his tone firm but filled with concern.

Marcus waved him off. "It is nothing, son. Just getting old."

But it was not anything.

The diagnosis

ONE PARTICULARLY GRUELING day, Marcus collapsed while helping carry groceries into the guesthouse. Devon, panicked, called for Daniel Sutton, who at once drove them both to the hospital. The diagnosis was devastating chronic obstructive pulmonary disease (COPD), a progressive illness worsened by years of exposure to harsh cleaning chemicals from his janitorial days and his old habit of smoking, long since kicked.

The doctor's prognosis was clear. Marcus would need to slow down, limit physical exertion, and adhere to a strict regimen of medication and oxygen therapy.

At first, Marcus tried to keep the diagnosis from Daniel and Elliot, determined to continue working. But the signs became impossible to ignore. One morning, as he prepared to drive Daniel into the city, he stumbled and had to steady himself against the car. Daniel caught sight of him and at once intervened.

"Marcus, enough," Daniel said, his voice a mix of frustration and concern. "You are not well. You need to rest."

"I can still do my job," Marcus insisted, though his trembling hands told a different story.

"You've done more than enough for this family," Daniel said gently. "It's time for you to take care of yourself."

Devon's Sacrifice

DESPITE DANIEL'S INSISTENCE, Marcus refused to step away completely. He felt an unspoken duty to the Suttons, a family who had given him and Devon so much. But his illness meant he could no longer handle the job alone.

Devon, now a young man with dreams of college and a bright future ahead of him, made a difficult choice. Seeing his father's declining health, he put his own ambitions on hold to take over the role of chauffeur.

"It's just temporary, Dad," Devon said when Marcus protested. "Until you're back on your feet."

Marcus knew better. He saw the way Devon buried his disappointment behind a forced smile.

The Final Days

MARCUS'S CONDITION continued to worsen over the next year. He grew weaker with each passing day, the vibrancy that once defined him now a distant memory. Devon took on more responsibilities, not only as the Suttons' chauffeur but as his father's caretaker.

On a quiet autumn evening, Marcus asked Jamal to sit with him outside the guesthouse. The air was cool, and the leaves were starting to turn.

"I'm proud of you, son," Marcus said, his voice raspy but steady. "I see the man you're becoming, and I know your mother would've been proud too."

Devon swallowed the lump in his throat. "I wouldn't be who I am without you, Dad."

Marcus smiled, his eyes glistening. "I know you have given up a lot for me. But promise me one thing, Devon. Do not let this... do not let my choices keep you from chasing your dreams. You are meant for more than this."

A week later, Marcus passed away peacefully in his sleep, leaving behind a legacy of hard work, integrity, and unconditional love.

The Decision to Stay On

AFTER MARCUS'S FUNERAL, Daniel Sutton approached Devon.

"Your father was a good man," Daniel said, his voice thick with emotion. "This estate won't be the same without him."

"He cared about you and Elliot a lot. About all of this."

Daniel placed a hand on Devon's shoulder. "You know, you do not have to stay, Devon. Your father would not have wanted you to feel tied to this place."

Devon thought about it, his father's words ringing in his ears. He had dreams—college, a career, a life beyond the walls of the Sutton estate. But he also felt a deep sense of loyalty to the family who had been there for him and his father.

"I'll stay for now," Devon said finally. "At least until you find someone else."

Daniel nodded, understanding the weight of Jamal's decision. "You will always have a place here, Devon. Always."

Though Devon stayed on as the Suttons' chauffeur, he quietly began to plan for his future, determined to honor his father's wishes and build a life that reflected Marcus's unwavering belief in his potential.

A Bond Forged in the Daily Commute

AFTER ELLIOTT'S DEPARTURE for Harvard, the dynamic within the Sutton household began to shift. With fewer familial obligations pulling him in different directions, Daniel Sutton found himself relying more on Devon Walker during his daily commute to and from Sutton Capital on Park Avenue. These moments together became more than just a ride—they evolved into an unexpected mentorship.

Daniel often used the quiet of the car ride to reflect on his business challenges, speaking candidly about the intricacies of financial markets, mergers and acquisitions, and the delicate balance of managing clients and staff. What surprised him was Devon's genuine interest. While Daniel initially saw the conversations to clear his own thoughts, Devon listened with intensity, often asking questions that proved a surprising level of understanding.

One crisp autumn morning, as they cruised through Manhattan's bustling streets, Daniel paused mid-thought and glanced in the rearview mirror. "Devon, you really have a knack for this stuff. You ever think about working in finance?"

Devon laughed nervously, glancing at Daniel through the mirror. "I mean, it fascinates me. I read the *Wall Street Journal* and the *Financial Times* whenever I get the chance, but I would not know where to start."

"Start with what you're already doing," Daniel replied. "You have more time during the day than most people could dream of. Why not make the most of it? Enroll in college. Study something related to the markets. Accounting, finance—something that can build a foundation."

Devon fell silent, his hands gripping the steering wheel as he considered the suggestion.

"I don't know," he admitted after a moment. "I've thought about it, but..."

"But what?" Daniel pressed, leaning forward slightly in his seat.

Devon hesitated. "I do not want to overstep. I mean, I am just your chauffeur, Mr. Sutton."

Daniel shook his head, his voice firm but kind. "You are not *just* anything, Devon. You have potential—more than you realize. I would not suggest it if I did not think you could handle it. And drop the 'Mr. Sutton.' Call me Daniel."

The words stayed with Devon long after he dropped Daniel off at the Sutton Capital building that morning. As he navigated the bustling city streets back toward Harlem, he could not shake the idea. College had always seemed out of reach—a distant dream overshadowed by the practical realities of life. But Daniel's encouragement felt different, as though someone finally saw something in him, he had not yet recognized in himself.

That evening, Devon sat at his modest kitchen table, flipping through brochures, and browsing the websites of local colleges. His heart raced as he read about Baruch College's programs in accounting and finance. It was a long shot, he thought, but it was worth trying.

The following day, during their morning commute, Devon broke the news to Daniel.

"I've decided to apply to Baruch for the fall," he said, glancing at Daniel through the rearview mirror.

A smile spread across Daniel's face. "That's the smartest decision you've made all year," he said, leaning back in his seat with a satisfied nod. "And if you need a recommendation, let me know. I will be happy to write one for you."

A New Beginning

BY THE TIME FALL ARRIVED, Devon was officially a college student, juggling his coursework with his duties as the Sutton family chauffeur. His days became a careful balance of early morning drives, classes in midtown Manhattan, and evenings poring over textbooks and assignments.

Daniel could not have been prouder. During their commutes, he began quizzing Devon on what he was learning, offering insights, and drawing connections to real-world scenarios at Sutton Capital.

"You know," Daniel remarked one morning, "you are learning faster than most of the junior analysts I have hired. You might have a future in this business after all."

Devon laughed but did not dismiss the compliment. Deep down, he felt a growing sense of confidence—a belief that he could build something of his own, though he kept those aspirations to himself for now.

Daniel and Devon's relationship had shifted. What had begun as a strictly professional arrangement had grown into something more—a genuine bond forged over shared interests and mutual respect. Daniel saw in Devon a younger version of himself: hungry for knowledge and determined to rise above his circumstances. Devon, in turn, admired Daniel's work ethic and wisdom, seeing him not just as an employer but as a mentor.

Little did either of them know, this period of growth and learning would set the stage for a rivalry neither could have expected.

A Circle of Influence

Devon's time at Baruch College was more than just an academic journey—it became the foundation for the relationships that would define his future. Between classes and long hours studying, Devon found himself forming connections with a few exceptional individuals who would later play pivotal roles in the success of BCG.

The first and most charismatic of these was **Joseph "Joe" Brown.** Joe was the kind of person who could light up a room with his confidence and humor. He had an innate charm that drew people to him, and his sharp mind for business only amplified his appeal. From their first meeting in a group project on corporate finance, Devon could tell that Joe had a natural knack for negotiation and networking.

"You've got the brains, Devon," Joe said one day after class as they grabbed coffee. "But every great operation needs a guy who can work the room, you know? That is where I come in."

Devon laughed but agreed. Joe's charisma was undeniable, and his ability to connect with people was something Devon knew he could rely on in the future.

The second key figure was **Ayesha Khan**, a brilliant strategist with a razor-sharp analytical mind. Ayesha was one of the top students in their finance cohort, often outpacing even the professors in her understanding of market trends and global economics. While Devon excelled in understanding financial systems and Joe thrived in relationship-building, Ayesha was the one who could see the big picture and map out a plan to achieve it.

Devon and Ayesha bonded over long nights in the library, dissecting case studies and bouncing ideas off each other. She had a disciplined approach that complemented Devon's growing entrepreneurial spirit.

"You're going places, Devon," Ayesha told him one night as they poured over a business model assignment. "But you need a solid plan. Vision without strategy is just dreaming."

Her words stuck with him, and Devon made a mental note: Ayesha was someone he needed in his corner.

The third person to join Devon's circle was **Michael "Mikey" Thompson**, a tech genius who had his finger on the pulse of the future. While not a finance major like the others, Mikey was studying computer science and had a passion for using technology to solve real-world problems.

Devon met Mikey at a campus seminar on the future of fintech. They struck up a conversation afterward, and it did not take long for Devon to see Mikey's potential.

"If you're serious about building something big, tech is the way to do it," Mikey said, pushing up his glasses. "The firms that don't adapt are going to get left behind."

Mikey's forward-thinking approach inspired Devon to think beyond traditional investment models. He realized that having someone like Mikey on his team could give him a competitive edge in a rapidly evolving industry.

A Turning Point

DEVON'S RELATIONSHIP with these three individuals deepened over time, and together, they became an unofficial team. Late-night study sessions turned into brainstorming sessions about future ventures. While the others might not have realized it yet, Devon was already envisioning a firm—a firm that would be unlike any other, built on the strengths of his growing network.

The Foundation

DEVON'S FRIENDSHIPS with Joe, Ayesha, and Mikey, became the foundation of his future success. Together, they would form the core team that helped Devon form Ballard Capital Group (BCG). Each brought unique skills and perspectives to the table, and their combined talents gave the firm a competitive edge that no one saw coming.

For Devon, this circle of influence was more than just a team—it was a family built on trust, ambition, and shared dreams. And as BCG began its ascent, it was clear that the bonds formed during those formative years were the key to its extraordinary success.

Pride and Promise

As Devon entered his senior year at Baruch College, the transformation was clear. Gone was the quiet, reserved young man who once felt out of place in the world of the wealthy. In his place stood someone brimming with confidence, driven by ambition, and armed with a deep understanding of the financial markets.

Daniel Sutton noticed the change. Each morning as Devon chauffeured him to Sutton Capital's sleek Park Avenue headquarters, Daniel found himself increasingly impressed by Devon's insights and maturity. Their conversations, which had once been casual exchanges about the weather or traffic, had evolved into deep discussions about global markets, corporate strategies, and investment opportunities.

One crisp autumn morning, as the Rolls-Royce glided through the city streets, Daniel looked over at Devon in the driver's seat.

"You've come a long way, Devon," Daniel said, his tone more paternal than businesslike.

Devon glanced at him in the rearview mirror, slightly surprised. "Thank you, Mr. Sutton. That means a lot coming from you."

Daniel smiled, adjusting his tie. "No, really. When I first suggested college, I knew you had potential. But I did not expect you to excel like this. Your professors rave about you, your grades are impeccable, and you have built a network of people who respect you. That's not easy, especially in this city."

Devon felt a swell of pride. He had worked tirelessly to balance his responsibilities as Daniel's chauffeur with his academic pursuits.

The long nights studying and the weekends spent networking instead of relaxing were finally paying off.

"It hasn't been easy," Devon admitted. "But I've had great advice along the way."

Daniel chuckled. "Well, you've earned it. I see a lot of my younger self in you, you know. Ambitious, willing to put in the work. That is a rare quality, Devon. Don't lose it."

A Growing Bond

THEIR BOND GREW STRONGER that year. Daniel began to see Devon as more than just an employee or a mentee. He admired Devon's tenacity and hunger for knowledge, and he often found himself rooting for the young man's success as if he were one of his own children.

Devon, in turn, valued Daniel's mentorship deeply. While his late father Marcus had been his foundation of strength and values, Daniel became a source of inspiration and guidance in navigating the world of business and finance.

"You're a natural, Devon," Daniel said one afternoon after Devon had shared his thoughts on an article in the *Financial Times*. "You've got instincts that can't be taught. If you ever wanted to intern at Sutton Capital after graduation, I'd be more than happy to make that happen."

The offer caught Devon off guard. "I'm honored, Mr. Sutton. I'll definitely think about it."

Daniel nodded, sensing the hesitation. "No pressure. I just want you to know the door is open. You're capable of achieving great things, Devon."

The Future Beckons

BY THE TIME DEVON STARTED his final semester, he had begun to envision a future that went beyond simply working for someone else. His confidence had grown, and with it, his ambitions. He spent his free time sketching out business ideas, brainstorming with his friends Joe, Ayesha, and Mikey, and studying market trends obsessively.

One evening, as Devon drove Daniel home, he shared his thoughts.

"I've been thinking a lot about the future," Devon began, his voice steady but thoughtful.

Daniel glanced up from his phone. "Oh? What is on your mind?"

"I want to build something of my own someday," Devon said. "A firm that's innovative, that adapts to the times. Something that brings a fresh perspective to the market."

Daniel smiled, a mixture of pride and curiosity. "That's a bold ambition, Devon. But boldness is what it takes to succeed in this industry. Just remember, it's not just about making money—it's about building something that lasts."

Devon nodded, taking the advice to heart. He knew the road ahead would not be easy, but he was ready for the challenge. And with Daniel's encouragement and the skills he had gained over the years, he felt more prepared than ever to take the first step toward his dreams.

For Daniel, seeing Devon's growth was a source of immense pride. He had always believed in Devon's potential, but now he saw the makings of a man who could change the game. As they pulled into the Sutton estate that night, Daniel gave Devon one last piece of advice.

"Whatever you do, Devon, don't settle. You have the talent, the drive, and the vision. The world is yours if you're willing to take it."

Devon parked the car and turned to Daniel with a determined smile. "I won't, Mr. Sutton. Thank you for everything."

Daniel stepped out of the car, pausing to pat Devon on the shoulder. "You're going to do great things, Devon. I just know it."

Devon watched as Daniel disappeared into the grand estate, the weight of his words settling over him. It was not just encouragement—it was a challenge. And Devon was ready to rise to it.

Trusting Instincts

ONE CRISP AUTUMN MORNING, as Devon pulled the Bentley out of the estate driveway, Daniel seemed unusually preoccupied. He was scanning through a thick packet of documents, his brow furrowed, and a hint of frustration in his usually composed demeanor.

"Everything okay, Mr. Sutton?" Devon asked, glancing at him in the rearview mirror.

Daniel sighed, placing the documents on the seat beside him. "Just a deal we're looking at. On paper, it looks perfect—great margins, robust growth potential, everything you would want. The team is practically salivating over it." He paused, rubbing his temples. "But something about it feels...off."

Devon could hear the hesitation in Daniel's voice. "Off, how? Numbers not adding up?"

"No, the numbers are fine. It is just a gut feeling. My instincts have kept me out of trouble more times than I can count. But trying to explain that to a room full of analysts...it is not easy," Daniel admitted.

Devon nodded, curious but aware of his place. "Sometimes instincts pick up what numbers don't."

Daniel chuckled softly. "Exactly. Well, we will see how it shakes out. Just one of those things."

Collaborative Insight

AFTER DROPPING DANIEL off at Sutton Capital's Park Avenue office, Devon headed to his classes at Baruch. During a break between lectures, he met up with Joe, Ayesha, and Mikey in the library.

"Dev, you've got that look," Joe said, leaning back in his chair.

"What look?" Devon asked, raising an eyebrow.

"The one where your mind's stuck on something," Ayesha chimed in, tapping her pen against her notebook. "Spill."

Devon grinned and pulled a few notes from his bag, summarizing what Daniel had shared about the deal. "It's not really my business, but Mr. Sutton's instincts are telling him something's wrong with this deal. I was thinking we could look at it. Just for fun."

Mikey raised an eyebrow. "For fun? You're talking about analyzing a multimillion-dollar deal."

"Come on, Mikey," Ayesha said, already opening her laptop. "It's a puzzle. And puzzles are fun."

The group got to work, digging into similar deals, analyzing market trends, and brainstorming potential red flags. As the minutes turned into hours, Devon felt the pieces begin to fall into place.

"Here it is," Joe said finally, pointing to a highlighted section in the notes they had compiled. "The valuation on this company looks inflated. They have a lot of short-term assets, but their long-term liabilities are a mess. If the market shifts even slightly, they're toast."

"And look at their client base," Ayesha added. "It's heavily concentrated. If they lose just one or two big clients, their revenue tanks."

Devon leaned back, impressed. "That's it. That is why it feels off. Everything hinges on too few variables. It's a house of cards."

Sharing the Findings

LATER THAT EVENING, as Devon picked up Daniel for the ride home, he decided to share what they had discovered.

"Mr. Sutton," Devon began hesitantly, "I was thinking about that deal you mentioned this morning. I hope you don't mind, but I looked into it during my break—with some friends from school."

Daniel raised an eyebrow, intrigued. "Oh? And what did you find?"

Devon explained their analysis, breaking down the inflated valuation, the concentrated client base, and the potential risks if the market shifted. He tried to keep his tone measured, but the excitement of the discovery seeped through.

Daniel listened intently; his expression thoughtful. When Devon finished, there was a long pause as Daniel mulled over the information.

"You've got sharp eyes, Devon," Daniel said finally. He reached for his phone and dialed a number.

"Alan, it's Daniel. Cancel the deal. I will explain tomorrow," he said briskly, then hung up.

Turning to Devon, he smiled, a rare warmth in his usually stoic demeanor. "Good catch, Devon. You might've just saved us millions."

Devon felt a mix of pride and humility. "Thank you, Mr. Sutton. I'm just glad I could help."

Daniel leaned forward and patted Devon on the shoulder. "You're not just helping. You are proving that you have the instincts for this business. Don't underestimate that."

As they continued the drive home, Devon could not help but feel a renewed sense of purpose. This was not about chauffeuring or studying anymore—this was about building something bigger, something that could one day rival even the great Sutton Capital.

A Bad Day

THE AUTUMN SUN HUNG low in the sky as Devon waited outside Sutton Capital for Daniel. The city buzzed around him, but Devon's focus was on his thoughts. Over the past few months, he had noticed subtle changes in Daniel: the quieter demeanor, the exhaustion that weighed him down even on the best days. Devon had a nagging feeling something was wrong, but he never pressed Daniel about it.

That evening, Daniel walked out of the building slower than usual, his briefcase swinging loosely in his hand. He smiled faintly when he saw Devon, but the smile did not reach his eyes. As he slid into the backseat of the car, Devon glanced at him in the rearview mirror. Something was off.

"How was your day, Mr. Sutton?" Devon asked, breaking the silence as he pulled away from the curb.

Daniel did not answer right away. He stared out the window, watching the city pass by in a blur of lights and motion. Finally, he said, "Bad day, son. Just a bad day."

Devon frowned. Daniel's voice was heavy, tinged with something deeper than fatigue. But he knew better than to pry. He nodded and kept driving, the hum of the engine filling the silence.

The News

ABOUT HALFWAY HOME, Daniel suddenly shifted in his seat. "Devon, pull over for a moment, will you?"

Devon's heart skipped a beat. "Of course, Mr. Sutton," he said, steering the car to the side of the road and putting it in park.

Daniel stepped out, leaning against the hood of the car, his head tilted back as if searching the darkening sky for answers. Devon hesitated for a moment before getting out and walking around to stand beside him.

"Is everything alright, Mr. Sutton?" Devon asked cautiously.

Daniel turned to face him; his expression unreadable. Then he placed both hands on Devon's shoulders, steadying himself as much as the young man before him.

"Devon," Daniel began, his voice uncharacteristically soft. "There's something I need to tell you. Something I've been keeping to myself."

Devon's chest tightened. "What is it?"

"I've been...battling an aggressive form of cancer," Daniel said slowly. "I've tried everything—the best doctors, the most advanced treatments—but today I got the final word. It is terminal. There's nothing more they can do."

For a moment, the words hung in the air, sharp and unyielding. Devon's face crumpled, and he stepped back, shaking his head. "No...no, no, no," he muttered, his voice cracking as he placed his hands over his face.

"Devon," Daniel said, stepping forward and pulling him into a firm embrace. "It's going to be okay. I have lived a good life. And I still have time to put things in order."

Devon sobbed into Daniel's shoulder, his resolve momentarily breaking. But Daniel's calm presence steadied him, and after a few moments, Devon nodded, wiping his eyes.

A Call to Family

THE REST OF THE DRIVE home was quiet, the weight of the revelation pressing down on them both. As Devon navigated the familiar roads, Daniel pulled out his phone and dialed Elliot, who was abroad on a year-long trip after his Harvard graduation.

"Elliot," Daniel said when his son answered. His voice was firm but kind. "I need you to come home as soon as possible. There's something important we need to discuss."

Elliot hesitated. "Dad, is everything okay?"

"We'll talk when you get here," Daniel replied. "Just promise me you'll come home."

"I'll be on the next flight," Elliot said, his voice tight with concern.

As Daniel hung up, Devon glanced at him in the mirror. "You told him?"

"Only enough to get him here," Daniel said with a faint smile. "Some things are better discussed face-to-face."

When they arrived at the estate, Daniel stepped out of the car, pausing to rest a hand on Devon's shoulder. "Thank you, son," he said quietly. "For everything."

Devon nodded; his throat too tight to respond. Watching Daniel Walk into the house, shoulders squared despite the weight he carried, Devon knew he would do everything in his power to honor the man who had become like a second father to him.

"Give Them Hell"

THE MORNING SUNBATHED the Sutton estate in a warm glow as Devon pulled the car around to the front of the house. The gravel crunched under the tires, and he parked just as Daniel stepped out of the house. Daniel moved with purpose, a smile on his face that belied the heavy news he had shared with Devon the night before.

Devon was still processing everything—Daniel's terminal diagnosis, the calm resolve in his voice, and the unshakable strength the man displayed even in the face of death. As Daniel slid into the back seat, he closed the door with a decisive click and said, "Let's go, son. No time to feel sorry for yourself. We've got a lot to do today."

Devon nodded, pulling out of the long driveway, the estate's towering oaks lining their path. As they reached the main road, Daniel leaned forward slightly. "So, son, let's talk about your future," he said, his tone light but focused.

Devon glanced at him in the mirror, his hands gripping the steering wheel tightly. "My future?"

"Yes," Daniel said firmly. "I've been watching you, Devon. You have a gift. I was going to bring you into the firm as an intern, but honestly, you are far beyond that. You're on par with some of my best analysts."

Devon's eyes widened. "I don't know about that, Mr. Sutton..."

"Trust me," Daniel interrupted, his voice steady. "You are. And after you graduate, I think you should get your license and start your own firm."

Devon blinked, momentarily stunned by the statement. "My own firm?"

"Yes," Daniel said, a faint smile tugging at his lips. "Now, don't get me wrong. Starting your own firm—especially as a Black man—is going to be extremely hard. You will face hurdles that others will not. But if anyone can do it, Devon, it's you."

Devon nodded, absorbing the weight of Daniel's words.

"What I suggest," Daniel continued, "is that you build it yourself with a core group of people you trust. A diverse team that can do more than one thing at a time. And one piece of advice I have for you..." He paused, locking eyes with Devon in the rearview mirror. "Don't put your name on the business. Don't let them see you coming."

Devon nodded again, his mind already racing with possibilities.

"And," Daniel added with a wry smile, "you're going to need to hire a white guy—at least initially. Someone who can walk into the rooms you can't."

Devon hesitated for a moment, then chuckled softly. "That was always the plan," he admitted.

Daniel's smile widened. "Smart man. A good place to start for you would be sports contracts. Young players are getting enormous deals these days, and they are looking for people they can trust with their money. I think you could slip right into that space and dominate."

He paused, leaning back against the seat, his smile turning into a proud grin. "Son, you're the Tiger Woods of the investment game."

Devon laughed, shaking his head. "Tiger Woods, huh?"

"That's right," Daniel said, his voice filled with warmth.

As they approached the Sutton Capital building, Daniel sat back, watching the cityscape unfold before them. The towering skyscrapers echoed his larger-than-life presence. When Devon stopped in front of the building, Daniel opened the door and stepped out.

Before walking inside, Daniel leaned down to the passenger window, his eyes locking onto Devon's. "Give them hell, son," he said firmly.

Devon smiled, the weight of his mentor's words sinking in. "I will, Mr. Sutton. I promise."

Daniel nodded, a satisfied look on his face, before turning and walking into the building, his silhouette disappearing into the grand lobby.

Devon sat in the car for a moment, watching him go. Then, with a newfound determination burning in his chest, he gripped the steering wheel and drove away, already planning the next steps of the future Daniel believed he could create.

Rifts and Rivalries

ELLIOT ARRIVED AT THE firm just past noon, stepping into the stately building that bore his family's legacy. His father, Daniel, was in a meeting with the board members, sharing the grim details of his health and the plans to transition leadership of Sutton Capital. Despite his declining health, Daniel spoke with calm authority, emphasizing the need for a seamless succession plan.

When the meeting concluded, Elliot knocked lightly on the door and entered, his usual confidence masking the nervousness he felt from the urgency in his father's tone earlier. Daniel stood as Elliot approached, embraced him tightly, and said, "I love you, son."

Elliot stepped back, alarmed by the rare display of emotion. "Dad... what's wrong?"

Daniel gestured to the couch, and they both sat down. With a deep breath, Daniel explained his terminal condition and the prognosis.

Elliot's world shattered. He stood up abruptly, pacing the room, his mind racing as tears welled up in his eyes. "No... no, Dad. There must be something they can do!"

Daniel stood and embraced him again, his voice steady but kind. "We will get through this, son. Together. I promise."

When Elliot finally calmed, they sat back down. Daniel took his hand and said, "Listen, son. We need to start planning. I need you to join the firm full-time. You are going to take over from me, and I want you to be ready. This is not how I wanted things to go, but I believe in you."

Elliot nodded slowly, his emotions still raw.

"You interned here during college, so you've seen how things work," Daniel continued. "But to utterly understand the heart of this company, I am embedding you with the senior management team. I want you to see, listen, take notes, and learn. These people helped me grow this business. Take their advice. Take their criticism. No one knows everything, Elliot, and you will not either. But if you are open to learning, you will succeed."

Moved by his father's faith, Elliot agreed and moved back to the family estate, determined to spend as much time as possible with Daniel. They began commuting to and from work together, bonding over shared memories and Daniel's endless lessons about the nuances of leadership.

Devon's Rise and Elliot's Resentment

MEANWHILE, DEVON WAS preparing for a milestone of his own. His graduation was only weeks away, and he was finishing his double major in Finance and Accounting with a perfect 4.0 GPA. Daniel, ever proud of Devon's accomplishments, often praised him, much to Elliot's quiet irritation.

For Elliot, it was hard to reconcile his father's health struggles with the admiration he showed toward Devon. The subtle comparisons between the two did not go unnoticed, and each word of praise for Devon felt like a slight against Elliot.

Despite his declining health, Daniel was adamant about attending Devon's graduation. On the day of the ceremony, he insisted on being there, refusing to let his condition stop him. Devon, seated among his classmates, beamed with pride when he saw Daniel in the audience. For a moment, the years of hardship and loss melted away, and he felt a profound sense of gratitude.

Elliot, however, seethed quietly. Seeing his father cheer so openly for Devon only deepened the wedge forming between them. The tension between the two men finally reached a breaking point one morning during their commute.

The Breaking Point

IT WAS AN ORDINARY morning, but the atmosphere in the car was tense. Elliot was pitching a deal to his father, describing plans to buy a struggling company, dismantle it, and sell off the assets. The strategy was profitable but ruthless, and it would result in hundreds of people losing their jobs.

Daniel sat in thoughtful silence as Elliot laid out the plan. In the rearview mirror, he caught Devon's expression—a subtle but unmistakable look of disapproval.

Finally, Daniel spoke. "Devon, you seem to disagree. What do you think?"

Elliot scoffed, his voice dripping with disdain. "What do you mean, *what do you think*? You are asking *him* for his opinion on this?"

Daniel raised a hand to stop him. "Wait, Elliot. I want to hear what he has to say."

With some hesitation, Devon began. "Well... I think dismantling the company might not be the best approach. What if, instead, you partner with the employees? Make them partial owners. Help them turn the company around by giving them a stake in its success. If the company thrives, the employees could eventually buy back your shares at a profit. No one loses their job, and you still make money in the process."

Daniel leaned back, considering the idea carefully. "That's... something worth exploring," he said, a spark of intrigue in his voice.

Elliot, however, was livid. "Are you kidding me?" he snapped, glaring at Devon. "This is business, not charity. You cannot just throw money at people and hope they fix things."

"Enough, Elliot," Daniel said firmly.

Furious, Elliot threw open the car door and stormed out, slamming it behind him. Daniel sighed deeply, watching his son's retreating figure.

Devon, still seated in the front, hesitated. "I am sorry, Mr. Sutton. I did not mean to—"

Daniel cut him off with a gentle smile. "Do not apologize, son. You were honest, and that is what matters."

The moment marked the final fracture in Elliot and Devon's already tenuous relationship. From that day forward, Elliot's resentment toward Devon hardened into something more—a simmering anger that would shape their future interactions in ways neither of them could yet foresee.

•

The Final Goodbye

BY THE END OF SUMMER, Daniel's health had deteriorated rapidly. Once the unshakable patriarch of Sutton Capital, he was now bedridden, his body worn down by the aggressive cancer he had fought with quiet determination. Despite his condition, Daniel remained mentally sharp, offering guidance to Elliot and Devon when they visited his room.

Elliot had taken over the day-to-day operations of the firm. Though he carried the family name and had been groomed for this role, the weight of responsibility often outpaced his readiness. Devon, meanwhile, was quietly preparing to move on. He had rented a ground-floor apartment in a brownstone in Harlem and was starting to think about office space and plans for his new firm.

Yet Devon could not bring himself to leave while Daniel was still alive. Daniel had been more than a mentor to him—he had become a father figure, a constant source of encouragement and belief in his potential. Devon decided he would wait, ensuring he could be there for Daniel in his final days.

The Last Conversation

ONE LATE EVENING, THE nurse attending to Daniel informed Devon that Daniel wanted to see him. With a heavy heart, Devon entered the dimly lit bedroom. The air was heavy with the scent of medicine and quiet determination. Daniel lay propped up against a mountain of pillows, his once-vibrant face now pale and gaunt. But his eyes still carried the spark of life.

"Come here, son," Daniel said, his voice a strained whisper.

Devon approached and sat beside the bed, unsure of what to say. Daniel reached for his hand, holding it firmly.

"I'm glad you're here," Daniel began. "There's something I need to say, and I need you to hear it."

Devon nodded; his throat tight.

"I want you to know how much I admire you," Daniel said, his words slow but deliberate. "You have grown into the man I always knew you could be. Watching you has been one of the great joys of my life."

Devon's eyes filled with tears. "Mr. Sutton, you have done so much for me. I would not be who I am without you."

Daniel gave a faint smile. "Nonsense. You had it in you all along. I just gave you a nudge." He gestured to the bedside table where an envelope rested. "That's for you."

Devon hesitated, then reached for the envelope and opened it. Inside was a check for $5 million.

His breath caught. "I... I cannot accept this," he stammered, his hands trembling.

"Yes, you can," Daniel said firmly. "This is how much I believe in you. I am investing in you, son. I know you will make it count."

Devon shook his head, overwhelmed. "This is too much. I never wanted anything from you. Your friendship, your belief in me—that is all I have ever needed."

Daniel's grip on his hand tightened. "You have already made me proud, Devon. Now do important things with this. Build something that lasts."

Tears streamed down both their faces as they embraced. When Devon finally pulled away, Daniel's voice softened. "You have been a son to me. And I will always be with you."

Devon nodded, unable to speak, and left the room, closing the door softly behind him.

The next morning, Daniel passed peacefully in his sleep.

A Parting of Ways

THE FUNERAL WAS A SOMBER affair, attended by the Sutton family, close friends, and colleagues who had been touched by Daniel's wisdom and kindness. Devon stayed in the background, offering quiet support to Elliot and the rest of the family.

After the service, Devon and Elliot met one last time at the guest house on the estate. The tension between them was palpable, the unspoken rivalry for Daniel's affection and trust still lingering in the air.

"I wanted to let you know," Devon began, "that I will be leaving. Moving back to the city."

Elliot nodded; his face unreadable. "That's probably for the best."

Devon hesitated, then added, "I would like for us to stay in touch. You are Daniel's son, and he always wanted us to—"

Elliot cut him off, his tone curt but polite. "I do not think that is necessary. We will both be busy."

Devon studied him for a moment, then nodded slowly. "Alright. Take care of yourself, Elliot."

Elliot gave a tight smile and extended a hand. They shook, but the gesture lacked warmth.

As Devon left the guest house and walked down the long driveway for the last time, he felt a mix of sadness and resolve. His time at Sutton Capital had ended, but Daniel's faith in him and the investment he had made gave him the courage to forge his own path.

Devon looked up at the clear autumn sky and whispered to himself, "I'll make you proud."

The next chapter of his life was about to begin.

The Birth of BCG

DEVON'S FIRST SUNDAY morning back in Harlem was a blend of nostalgia and ambition. After years of navigating Manhattan's corporate world, returning to the familiar streets of his youth brought a strange mix of comfort and longing. He woke early, dressed, and grabbed a handball from his desk—a relic from his childhood—and walked to the diner on 135th Street for breakfast.

After eating, Devon headed to the park near the handball courts where he and his father had spent countless mornings. Sitting on the bench, he reflected on those days when his father taught him the game, blending life lessons with the rhythm of the ball hitting the wall.

About thirty minutes later, a tall, fit man in his late fifties entered the courts. The man, whom Devon later learned was George Lewis, started playing a solo game. He noticed the ball in Devon's hand and called out, "You play?"

Devon nodded, and the two began a series of games. George won all three, each closer than the last. Sweaty and tired, they sat together on the bench, exchanging stories.

"I'm George," the man said, extending a hand.

"Devon. You have a hell of a game, George."

George chuckled. "You are not bad yourself. It is rare to see a young guy like you out here playing handball. Most are playing basketball."

Devon smiled. "My father taught me. He loved this game. Said it taught patience and precision."

George nodded. "What was his name?"

"Marcus Walker," Devon replied.

George's eyes lit up. "Walker? Marcus Walker? I remember him! He used to dominate these courts back in the day. I could never beat him."

Devon's smile turned wistful. "That was my dad. He passed away a few years ago."

George offered his condolences, and their conversation shifted. George asked about Devon's life and future. Devon shared his dreams of starting an investment firm in Harlem.

Impressed, George reached into his pocket and handed Devon a business card. "George Lewis. I own a building on 125th Street. Stop by my office tomorrow. I might have just the space you are looking for."

Securing the Foundation

THE NEXT MORNING, DEVON visited George's office at 55 W. 125th Street. Walking into the newly renovated lobby, Devon felt a surge of excitement. He was greeted by George's secretary, who led him into a spacious, modern office.

After discussing Devon's vision for his firm, George took him to the seventh floor to show him an available office space. The room was perfect—modest yet professional, with enough potential to grow into something great.

"What do you think?" George asked.

Devon smiled. "It's perfect."

Back in George's office, they completed the lease. As George handed him the keys, he asked, "What's the name of your firm?"

Devon paused, the weight of the moment settling over him. Finally, he said, "Ballard Capital Group. BCG."

Assembling the Team

THAT EVENING, DEVON stood outside the building, holding the keys to his future. He called Joe, Ayesha, and Mikey, asking them to meet him in front of the building at 7 PM. He also asked Joe to bring Ben Keene, a friend Devon had met through Joe.

Ben was exactly the kind of person Devon needed—a tall, charming, and down-to-earth white man who could seamlessly navigate rooms filled with old money clients. Devon understood the unfortunate reality that there were places Ben could go where Devon could not, at least not yet.

When the group arrived, Devon held up the keys with a grin. They followed him upstairs to the new office, where an old conference table and chairs were the only furnishings. Devon ordered Chinese food, and as they ate, he began outlining his vision.

"Here's the plan," he began. "Joe, you will focus on sports contracts. You already have connections in the entertainment industry, and this is your wheelhouse. Ben, you are our gateway to old money. I know you understand why you are here. There are rooms you can walk into that I cannot—for now."

Ben nodded, completely at ease. "Got it."

"Mikey," Devon continued, "your sector is tech. I want you ahead of the curve. Look at emerging technologies, figure out what is next, and develop a trading algorithm that will give us a competitive edge. We need speed and precision."

Turning to Ayesha, he added, "You and I will focus on mergers and acquisitions. But we are not tearing companies apart for profit. We are going to partner with struggling businesses, turn them around, and make them sustainable."

The team listened intently, their excitement growing. Joe finally broke the silence. "This is all great, but... where's the money coming from?"

Devon smiled and opened his laptop, revealing an account balance of $8.5 million. The room fell silent.

"Where did this come from?" Ayesha asked, wide-eyed.

Devon explained: the $5 million Daniel had gifted him, a $2 million insurance payout from his father, and $1.5 million he had earned through personal investments.

"I've been preparing for this moment for a long time," Devon said. "Now I am ready. The question is—are you?"

The team looked at one another, then back at Devon. One by one, they nodded. Joe leaned back in his chair and said, "Let's go."

Devon smiled, the weight of his journey lifting just enough to reveal a flicker of triumph. The team was in place, the foundation laid. Now it was time to build something extraordinary.

A Bold Move for BCG

WITHIN A FEW MONTHS, BCG's office was a hive of activity. The team had grown exponentially, with each department focusing on their specific roles and goals. Devon's vision was finally taking shape.

One morning, Devon called Ayesha into his office to discuss a potential opportunity that could transform the firm.

"I need you to look into a company called Ryder Manufacturing," Devon began, sliding a folder across the desk. "It is a tire company upstate. A few years ago, a Japanese firm bought them with plans to expand. But now, they are shutting down operations. That is 1,200 people out of work, and it is going to devastate the town."

Ayesha scanned the file. "You're thinking about saving it?"

Devon nodded. "If we can, it will be a huge win—not just for the company but for the community. This could put us on the map. I need you to assemble a management team and start formulating a plan."

The Ryder Deal

WHILE AYESHA WORKED on assembling the team, Devon reached out to the parent company in Japan. After a few rounds of negotiations, they presented an offer: the plant was on the table if BCG could handle the transition.

Devon called a meeting with the newly assembled management team and laid out the framework for their plan. Once completed, he took the plan directly to Ryder's employees. In a packed town hall, Devon explained his vision: BCG would buy the plant, and the workers would take part-ownership alongside BCG. This partnership would ensure their investment in the company's success.

The employees voted unanimously to move forward. BCG gave a counteroffer to the Japanese firm, which was accepted. Devon and the team wasted no time installing new leadership and implementing changes.

Within a year, Ryder Manufacturing was back in operation, turning a profit and restoring stability to the town. The deal not only saved the company but also set up BCG as a leader in transformative mergers and acquisitions.

The Domino Effect

NEWS OF RYDER'S SUCCESS spread quickly. Companies began approaching BCG, seeking their ability in turnarounds. Deal after deal, BCG carved out a niche, becoming the go-to firm for ethical and sustainable business rescues.

This success fueled growth across all divisions:

- **Ben's team** started landing high-net-worth clients, solidifying their reputation among affluent investors.

- **Joe's team** attracted more athletes and entertainers, securing lucrative sports and media deals.

- **Mikey's team** developed an ultramodern trading algorithm that outperformed competitors and made early investments in promising tech startups.

The firm grew so rapidly that they soon needed the entire seventh floor of their building.

Lunch with George

ONE DAY, DEVON INVITED George Lewis to lunch at Sylvia's to discuss the firm's rapid expansion.

Over a plate of fried chicken and collard greens, George smiled proudly. "You have done amazing things, Devon. I always knew you would. What is on your mind?"

"We're outgrowing our space," Devon admitted. "I'm thinking ahead and want to explore options for the next phase of our growth."

George leaned back and grinned. "I might have just the thing."

He gestured out the window toward the boarded-up block at the corner of Lenox Avenue and 125th Street. "You see that lot? It has been sitting there for years. There is a plan in place to develop a mixed-use building—offices and residential space. All we need is a group to buy the property and see it through. I want you to be part of it."

Devon did not hesitate. "I'm in."

A New Home

WITHIN SIX MONTHS, construction began on the new building. Devon quietly joined George's investment group, securing partial ownership of the project. He did not mention his involvement to the team, focusing instead on BCG's day-to-day operations.

One day, however, Ben and Joe got off the train at 125th Street and noticed a large sign on the construction site: **"Future Home of BCG."**

Shocked, they rushed to the office and burst into Devon's room.

"Devon, is it true?" Joe asked, out of breath.

Devon looked up from his desk. "Is what true?"

Ben pointed out the window. "That building across the street. Do you own it?"

Devon sighed and smiled. "Yes."

Joe and Ben exchanged high-fives, laughing. "Man, you've been holding out on us!" Joe said.

Devon shrugged, amused. "Get back to work. We have deals to close."

As they left, Devon leaned back in his chair, gazing out at the construction site. For the first time, he allowed himself a moment to appreciate how far they had come—and how much further they were going to go.

A Night Out

IT WAS A QUIET SATURDAY evening when Devon sat at his desk, surrounded by paperwork. His focus was intense, as it always was when it came to his work. Suddenly, his phone rang—it was Joe.

"What are you doing tonight?" Joe asked.

"Working," Devon replied without looking up.

"No, not tonight," Joe said firmly. "I am coming to get you. It cannot be all work all the time. You need to have some fun."

"Joe, I have things to do—" Devon started, but Joe cut him off.

"Nope. I will see you in thirty minutes."

Thirty minutes later, Devon was standing outside his office when a sleek black limo pulled up. Joe rolled down the window.

"Get in," he said, grinning.

"Where are we going?" Devon asked, reluctant.

"Don't worry about it," Joe said, laughing. "Just trust me."

A Chance Meeting

THE LIMO DROVE THEM to Brooklyn, stopping at a chic rooftop bar with twinkling string lights and a breathtaking view of the Manhattan skyline. Joe led Devon through the crowd, introducing him to a group of friends he had been meeting.

Among them was a striking woman who at once caught Devon's attention. Her name was **Imani Reid**, a journalist for *The New York Times*. She had a warm smile, intelligent eyes, and a presence that was both captivating and grounded.

"Devon Walker," he introduced himself, shaking her hand.

"Imani Reid," she replied, smiling.

The conversation between them flowed effortlessly. They talked about everything—her work in journalism, his growing firm, their shared love of Harlem, and even their favorite books and foods. Devon, who was usually reserved and careful with his words, found himself opening in a way he had not in years.

By the end of the evening, they exchanged numbers, and Devon felt something he had not felt in a long time: excitement that was not tied to business.

Falling In Love

OVER THE NEXT FEW MONTHS, Devon and Imani became inseparable. They explored Harlem together, spent evenings cooking meals in her cozy apartment, and talked about their hopes and dreams late into the night.

Imani's sharp wit and grounded perspective complemented Devon's ambitious drive. She challenged him to see things from new angles, while he introduced her to the world of high finance and strategy. They balanced each other perfectly, building a bond that grew stronger with each passing day.

The Future

IMANI QUICKLY BECAME a fixture in Devon's life, not only as his partner but as his confidante and muse. Devon, who had always envisioned his future with calculated precision, suddenly saw it in a new light—with Imani by his side.

Years later, she would become his wife and the mother of his children, a partner in every sense of the word. But on that night, as they sat together under the Brooklyn skyline, Devon realized something profound: for the first time, his life felt complete.

The Confrontation

Fred and Amanda Carlson were no strangers to Manhattan's elite social circles. Coming from generations of old money, live comfortably on the cities upper echelon. They felt their current firm was failing them. That is when they reached out to Ben Keene, the charming young face of BCG who had quickly become a trusted adviser to many in their social circles. They agreed to meet at the Old Homestead Steakhouse in downtown Manhattan, a place where the city's wealthiest dine and deals are over rare cuts and fine wine The evening began with polite conversation over appetizers. Ben ever so professional listened intently attentively as Fred and Amanda shared their concerns about their current firm. As the discussion turned to potential strategies a familiar figure approached their table, Elliot Sutton. Fred and Amanda greeted Elliot warmly he had managed your portfolio for for years and thought they were their relationship had grown distant there was still a veneer of cordiality. "Elliot, Fred exclaimed standing to shake his hand, this is Ben Keene from BCG, we are exploring some opportunities with him." Elliot turned to Ben offering a firm handshake "Ben Keene" he said his tone neutral but his eyes scanning the young man's intently Ben smiled politely," pleasure to meet you, Elliott." There was a flicker of recognition in Elliot's eyes "that uptown firm, right?" "That is correct" Ben replied. Elliott lingered lingered for a moment before turning to Fred and Amanda, "might we have a word" Elliot asked Fred nodded, Ben excuse himself from the to the restroom leaving Fred Amanda and Elliot at the table. As soon as Ben was out of earshot Elliot leaned in "Fred are you leaving us?" Fred spoke plainly we are exploring our options. "Elliot your firm has gotten stagnant there is no creativity no growth. Friends of ours moved their portfolio to BCG are seeing results so yes, we are looking for alternatives." Elliot's face tightened but he forced a thin smile "well that is your prerogative" he said rising to leave he shook Fred's hand. In the restroom Elliot cornered Ben, "how dare you poach my clients" he demanded. Ben's voice low but sharp met his gaze "we do not poach clients Elliot; they came to us. If they are not happy with your service that is not our fault, we just offer them a solution." Elliot looked Ben in the eyes but there was nothing more to say, he turned and stormed out in anger. The next morning Elliot was still stewing over the encounter, he called his assistant to the office. "Get me everything you can on BCG I want to know who they are where they came from and how they are pulling clients like Fred Carlson." A few hours later his assistant returned with a thick report. what did you find Elliot asked? The assistant began summarizing. "BCG started small focus on mergers and acquisition particularly rescuing struggling companies. Their success with Ryder Manufacturing put them on the map and since then they have been expanding rapidly, they have built divisions for sports contracts, tech investments and even developed a proprietary trading algorithm that's outperforming competitors." "Who owns BCG?" The assistant hesitated before answering, "the CEO and majority owner is a man named Devon Walker." Elliot froze. "Let me see that" he demanded snatching the report. His eyes scanned the page until he found the name Devon Walker and then a photograph. It was him. Elliot sank into his chair. The report trembling in his hands, it cannot be he murmured, but there was no mistake. Devon Walker the boy he had dismissed and the son of the man he barely knew was now the CEO of one of the fastest growing investment firms in New York. For the first time in years Elliot Sutton felt truly shaken.

THE SAUDI FUND

The next morning Ben stepped into Devon's office, his expression a mix of excitement and curiosity. Devon, seated at his desk, glanced up from his paperwork.

"What's up, Ben?" Devon asked, setting his pen down.

Ben leaned back in his chair. "First off, we landed the Carlson account. Fred and Amanda officially signed on this morning."

Devon nodded approvingly. "Good work. Anything else?"

Ben hesitated for a moment, then added, "I ran into Elliot last night at the Old Homestead."

Devon raised an eyebrow. "Oh? How would that go?"

Ben recounted the encounter, including Elliot's accusations in the restroom. Devon listened, his expression calm.

When Ben finished, Devon shrugged. "Let him stew. If his clients are coming to us, that is on him, not us. What else is on your plate?"

Ben smirked, appreciating Devon's composure. "How do you feel about doing business with the Saudis?"

Devon looked intrigued. "The Saudis? What do you mean?"

Ben explained, "There is a conference at the Ritz-Carlton next week. The Saudi Royal Fund is looking for a new firm to manage their portfolio, and BCG was one of the ten firms selected to attend."

Devon leaned forward; his interest piqued. "They selected us?"

Ben nodded. "It is important. The fund is massive billions. This could take us to the next level."

Devon smiled. "Alright. Set it up. We are ready for this."

The Ritz-Carlton Conference

THE FOLLOWING WEEK, Devon and Ben arrived at the Ritz-Carlton, dressed sharply, and radiating confidence. The conference room was already bustling with representatives from some of the most prestigious firms in the world. Ben pointed out a few familiar faces, introducing Devon as they navigated the room.

It was not long before Elliot Daniels walked in with his team. His gaze at once locked onto Devon, and for a moment, their eyes met. Devon started to make his way over, but Elliot turned abruptly and walked in the opposite direction.

Devon paused, a faint smirk tugging at his lips. "Still holding a grudge," he murmured to Ben, who chuckled.

As everyone took their assigned seats, the Saudi representatives began their presentation. They explained their goal of finding a dynamic, innovative firm to manage their royal fund. The ten firms in the room had been handpicked based on their performance, reputation, and vision.

The stakes were clear. Each firm had seven days to send a proposal, and the Saudis would announce their decision within ten days.

The Announcement

TEN DAYS LATER, ELLIOT Daniels sat in his office, anxiously awaiting the decision. When his phone finally rang, he snatched it up.

"Daniels," he answered sharply.

The voice on the other end delivered the news: his firm had not been selected.

Elliot's face darkened. "Who got it?" he demanded.

"BCG," the voice replied.

Elliot slammed the phone down, the sound echoing in his office. He stood, walking to the window, his jaw clenched as he stared out over the city.

At the same time, Devon stood before his entire staff at BCG's Harlem headquarters. He held up his hands to quiet the buzz of excitement in the office.

"I have an announcement," he began, his voice steady but brimming with pride. "We've just signed our newest client—the Saudi Royal Fund."

The room fell silent for a split second, then erupted into cheers and applause.

"This is a game-changer," Devon continued, his voice rising above the celebration. "This is what we have been working for. We are not just here to play the game—we are here to lead it."

As the cheers grew louder, Devon allowed himself a moment to smile. BCG had arrived on the global stage, and there was no turning back.

The Toast

ELLIOT SUTTON POURED himself a drink, the amber liquid swirling in the crystal glass. He sat heavily on the sofa, his gaze falling on a framed photo of his father on the table. Raising his glass, he toasted the image.

"You tried to tell me," Elliot said quietly. "You were right. I just would not listen."

After a moment of silence, he picked up his phone and dialed.

Across town, Devon sat in his office, leaning back in his chair, reflecting on the day's triumph. His phone rang. Glancing at the screen, he saw Elliot's name and picked up, intrigued.

"Devon," Elliot began, his voice measured yet sincere. "Congratulations on the Saudi contract."

"Thank you," Devon replied cautiously. The words sounded heartfelt.

Elliot hesitated before continuing, his tone softening. "I also want to apologize—for everything. The way I treated you over the years... it was not fair. It was jealousy. Jealousy over how my father felt about you. I could not see it then, but I do now."

Devon was silent, unsure how to respond.

"I want to thank you," Elliot continued.

"Thank me?" Devon asked, surprised.

"Yes. For reigniting something in me. A fire that I thought was gone—the fire my father always believed I had but I could not find. Watching what you have built gave me the push I needed to treat this firm with the respect my father always did." Elliot's voice cracked slightly. "I lost that somewhere along the way."

Devon exhaled deeply. "I don't know what to say."

"Maybe one day," Elliot added, "we could get together, share a drink, and reminisce about the good times. Because, despite everything, there were good times when we were younger."

Devon smiled faintly. "I would like that very much. It is good to hear from you, Elliot."

The two men exchanged a quiet goodbye, hanging up with a newfound understanding between them.

New Beginnings

IN THE YEARS THAT FOLLOWED, BCG moved into its sleek new headquarters, its reputation solidifying as one of the most respected firms in New York. Devon and Imani settled into the penthouse apartment above the building, where they welcomed their first child, a boy they named Marcus, after Devon's father.

Elliot, too, found his focus again, revitalizing his father's struggling firm and steering it toward renewed success.

One Saturday afternoon, the elevator doors opened into Devon and Imani's penthouse. Elliot stepped out, carrying a bottle of scotch, and accompanied by his fiancée, Karen. Imani was in the living room, holding baby Marcus, her smile brightening as she greeted their guests.

Elliot handed the bottle to Karen and extended his arms. "Let me see my nephew," he said with a grin.

Imani handed the baby to him, and Elliot held the boy gently, his face softening.

On the balcony, Devon stood watching the scene with a sense of pride and contentment. He knew their fathers, Marcus, and Daniel, were looking down on them, smiling at the unity and growth their sons had achieved.

A moment later, Karen and Imani took Marcus into the kitchen, leaving Elliot and Devon alone on the balcony. Elliot joined him, holding two glasses of scotch. He handed one to Devon, and they clinked glasses.

"To life," Elliot said, gazing out over the skyline.

Devon nodded, taking a sip. "Life is good."

Elliot patted him on the back. "Glad I'm here."

Devon smiled, his heart full. "Wouldn't want it any other way."

The two men stood there, side by side, looking out over the city they would both risen to conquer—together, in their own ways.

The End.